The Junior Novelization

Published in the United States by Random House Children's Books, a division of Random House, Inc., New York, and in Canada by Random House of Canada Limited, Toronto, in conjunction with Disney Enterprises, Inc. RANDOM HOUSE and colophon are registered trademarks of Random House, Inc.
Library of Congress Control Number: 2006940604
ISBN: 978-0-7364-2439-4
www.randomhouse.com/kids
Printed in the United States of America
10 9 8 7 6 5 4 3 2 1

The Junior Novelization

Adapted by Kitty Richards

Random House New York

# Prologue

*Although each of the world's countries would like to dispute this fact, the French know the truth: the best food in the world is made in France. The best food in France is made in Paris, and the best food in Paris, some say, was made by Chef Auguste Gusteau. Gusteau's restaurant was the toast of Paris, booked five months in advance, and his dazzling ascent to the top of fine French cuisine made his competitors envious. He was the youngest chef ever to achieve a five-star rating.*

*As Gusteau himself once said, "Good food is like music you can taste, color you can smell.*

*There is excellence all around you; you need only to be aware to stop and savor it."*

*Chef Gusteau's cookbook,* Anyone Can Cook!, *climbed to the top of the bestseller list. But not everyone celebrated its success.*

*Anton Ego, noted food critic, was one of the naysayers. "Amusing title,* Anyone Can Cook!,*" he once said with a sneer. "What's even more amusing is that Gusteau actually seems to believe it. I, on the other hand, take cooking seriously, and no, I don't think 'anyone' can do it."*

*But who was right? Was it true that anyone—regardless of upbringing, training, or type of kitchen—could cook a meal fine enough to satisfy even a notoriously impossible-to-please man like Anton Ego?*

*Turn the page, and we will try to get to the bottom of this culinary quandary. . . .*

Remy had a lot going for him. He was young and talented. He lived in an old farmhouse in the rolling green hills of the French countryside. And he had a rare and remarkable skill.

So why was Remy so unhappy?

It all came down to one thing: Remy was a rat. And life for a rat, even in the French countryside, was very hard. There was a lot of sneaking around. A lot of stealing. And a lot of eating—mostly garbage. It made Remy sick to his stomach.

You see, Remy had a special gift—highly developed senses of taste and smell. There was nothing he liked better than finding special ingredients, dreaming up recipes, and creating new flavor combinations.

Here's how talented Remy was: When a regular rat spotted a half-eaten napoleon—a decadent layered puff pastry—he thought, *Food! Eat it now!* (To put that into perspective, when a regular rat saw a rotten banana peel, he also thought, *Food! Eat it now!*) But when Remy spotted a half-eaten napoleon, he paused. He closed his eyes, took a great sniff of the delicate pastry, and relished the concerto of delectable tastes. Almost as if in a dream, he began to identify the many ingredients. "Hmm . . . flour, eggs, sugar, vanilla bean . . ." Then he would pause for a moment and add, "Oh, small twist of lemon."

Remy's big brother Emile might not have been quite as discerning, but he knew talent when he saw it, and he was in awe of Remy. But their father, Django, the leader of their rat clan, had two words to say about Remy's talent: "so" and "what."

That is, he did until Remy sniffed just as

Django was about to take a big bite out of an apple core. Remy smelled something funny—very funny. So he lunged at his father, knocking the apple out of his hands.

"Whoa!" cried Remy. *"Don't eat that!"*

"Wh-what's going on here?" shouted Django.

Remy sniffed the air, caught the scent, and followed it to a tarp in the corner of the yard. He lifted the tarp. Underneath was a can of rat poison!

Suddenly, Django didn't think Remy's talent was so useless. And Remy was finally feeling good about his gift—until he found out what his dad had in store for him.

Remy's new job was to smell food all day. And not just any food—rotten food. Day in and day out, a seemingly endless line of rats filed past him, holding up rank scraps of food for him to smell. That's right. He was Chief Poison Checker for his clan.

Remy sniffed. A moldy crust of bread. A slimy bit of plum. A bite of beef with a slight green tinge to it. "Clean . . . clean . . . clean . . ."

The rats moved on. Their scraps would be added to the food pile, to be served later that night at dinner.

Remy sniffed again. A deflated grape. Some curdled milk. A wilted piece of lettuce. "Clean-errific . . . clean-erino . . . close to godliness . . ." Remy was bored to tears.

Django watched his son proudly. "Now don't you feel better, Remy?" he asked. "You've helped a noble cause."

Remy stared at his father in disbelief. "Noble?" he spluttered. "We're thieves, Dad. And what we're stealing is—let's face it—garbage."

"It isn't stealing if no one wants it," Django said with a shrug.

Remy rolled his eyes. "If no one wants it, why are we stealing it?"

Django turned and walked away. "We are not having this argument again!" he called over his shoulder.

Later that night, in the farmhouse attic, the rats were all contentedly munching on garbage . . . er, their dinner. All except Remy, of course. He had a motto: "If you are what you eat, then only eat the good stuff."

But Django thought differently. He had a motto, too, and he turned to Remy and shared it with him. "Food is fuel. You get picky about what you put in the tank, your engine is gonna die. Now, shut up and eat your garbage."

Remy was not convinced. "If we're going to be thieves," he argued, "why not steal the good stuff in the kitchen—where nothing is poisoned?"

That made Django angry. "First of all, we are *not* thieves. Secondly, stay out of the kitchen and away from the humans. It's dangerous."

*Well,* thought Remy, *what my father doesn't know won't hurt him.*

The next day, Remy slowly and silently sneaked into the farmhouse kitchen. The television was on, tuned to a cooking channel. On-screen, Gusteau, the portly, famous chef, was busy cooking another masterpiece. The old woman who lived in the house was fast asleep in the television's glow.

Remy stared at the TV with glee. As a rat, he knew he was supposed to hate humans. But there was something about them. They didn't just survive; they discovered, they created. And just look what they did with food!

From his perch on the counter, Remy noticed a well-worn copy of Gusteau's cookbook, *Anyone*

*Can Cook!*, propped up next to the stove. And to his delight, right next to it was a plate of leftover fruits and cheeses. *Bingo!* thought Remy.

"Good food is like music you can taste, color you can smell," the great chef said from the TV. "There is excellence all around you. You need only be aware to stop and savor it."

Remy reached over to the cheese plate and picked up a small slice. He closed his eyes and took a bite. Oh, yeah—delicious. Gusteau was right!

The cheese still in his mouth, Remy reached over and picked up an apple slice. He took a bite and nearly wept with pleasure. Each flavor was totally unique. But combine one flavor with another . . . and something *new* was created.

Remy was unceremoniously brought back to reality when the old woman reached over and turned on her lamp. She was awake!

Remy gasped. Quick as a flash, he ran to the window and jumped outside.

But he couldn't help turning back for one last

look. He had conquered the kitchen. And now he had a secret life.

The only one who knew Remy's secret was his brother Emile. One late afternoon, as Remy was hurrying through the field behind the farmhouse, he ran into Emile rummaging through some garbage. "Psst! Hey, Emile!" Remy called.

Emile stopped and held up the remnants of someone's brown-bag lunch. "I found a mushroom!" Remy exclaimed. "Come on," he told his brother. "You're good at hiding food. Help me find a good place to put this!"

Emile dragged the greasy paper bag while Remy walked upright, cradling his mushroom.

All of a sudden, a rich and enticing scent caught Remy's attention. Could it possibly be coming from the bag his brother was carrying? "What have you got there?" he asked Emile. Then he disappeared inside the bag.

"Oh!" He chuckled delightedly. "Cheese? You

found cheese? And not just any cheese—Tomme de Chèvre de Pays! That would go beautifully with my mushroom! And . . . and . . . !"

Remy spotted exactly what he needed—rosemary and sweetgrass. He grabbed a pawful of each.

Emile wasn't quite sure what to make of this. "Well, throw it on the pile, I guess," he said. "And then we'll, you know . . ."

Remy stared at his brother in disbelief. "But we don't want to throw this in with the garbage! This is special!"

Emile was flabbergasted. Remy knew the rules as well as any other rat in their clan. "But we're supposed to return to the colony before sundown," said Emile. "Or Dad's gonna . . ."

"Emile!" Remy shouted. Then he took a deep breath and regained his composure. "There are possibilities unexplored here. We've got to cook this. Now, exactly *how* we cook this is the real question."

That was when Remy looked at the farmhouse

and noticed the smoking chimney. He grinned. "Yeah. Come on!"

Moments later the two brothers sat on the farm-house roof. Emile stared at Remy, not knowing what to make of this situation. Remy had skewered the mushroom and the cheese onto a bent metal rod, which he held over the smoking chimney.

Just then, lightning flickered in the distance. Shortly thereafter came a boom of thunder.

"That storm is getting closer," Emile said nervously. "Hey, Remy, you think that maybe we shouldn't be so close to—"

But his warning came too late. *Crack!* A bolt of lightning hit the TV antenna on the roof and the metal rod in Remy's hand, its force knocking both rats off the rooftop and down into a puddle.

They lay there, soaking and dazed, their electrified fur smoking and sticking straight up. Emile was not terribly surprised to see that Remy had kept the rod aloft so that his precious mushroom would be kept dry. The mushroom had been transformed into a curious puffed-out shape.

"Whoa, ohhh," Remy moaned. Then he took a bite of his mushroom. "Ohhhh, you gotta taste this!" He smacked his lips in excitement. "It's got this kind of taste, don't you think? What would you call that flavor?" Remy asked his brother.

"Lightningy?" Emile suggested.

"Yeah, it's lightningy!" Remy exclaimed. His mind was racing. He took another bite of the mushroom. "I know what this needs! Saffron! A little saffron would make this!"

"Why do I get the feeling . . . ," said Emile.

The two rats finished his sentence together: ". . . it's in the kitchen."

Emile did not like the sound of that one bit.

"Relax," said Remy. "It's just after sundown. The old lady is napping in front of the TV this time of day. Come on!"

Supportive older brother that he was, Emile followed Remy into the farmhouse. But in his heart he knew that this was a bad idea.

In the kitchen, Remy happily rummaged through the spices while Emile stared nervously at the old lady, who was fast asleep in front of the TV. As usual, it was tuned to the cooking channel.

*Saffron . . . saffron . . . where is the saffron?* Remy located tarragon, allspice, sage, basil and dill. But the saffron was nowhere to be found.

Emile was starting to panic. “Not good. Don’t like it. She’s gonna wake up.”

“I’ve been down here a million times,” said Remy. “She turns on the cooking channel, and *boom*. Never wakes up.”

“You’ve been here a million times?”

Remy ignored his brother. "I'm telling you, saffron will be just the thing. Gusteau swears by it."

Emile was lost. "Okay, who's Gusteau?" he asked.

"Just the greatest chef in the world," Remy replied. He pushed aside some cookbooks, revealing the old woman's copy of *Anyone Can Cook!* "Gusteau wrote this cookbook."

Emile stared at his brother. "Wait a minute. *You read?*"

Remy bit his lip. "Well, not excessively," he said, embarrassed.

"Oh, man," Emile groaned. "Does Dad know?"

Remy laughed. "You could fill a book—a *lot* of books—with things Dad doesn't know. And they have . . . which is why I read. Which is also our secret."

Emile was upset. "I don't like secrets. All this cooking and reading and TV-watching while we read and cook. It's like you're involving me in a crime. And I let you. Why do I let you?"

Remy barely even heard his brother. That saffron had to be somewhere!

Meanwhile, above their heads, the rat colony streamed into the dark attic. It was dinnertime. Django watched as each rat carried food from the compost heap and tossed it into a pile in the center of the room. But he was distracted. *What's taking those kids so long?* he wondered.

At last! Remy located a tiny tin of saffron and held it up as if it were a rare jewel. "Ah, Aquila saffron. Italian. Gusteau says it's excellent. Good thing the old lady is a food lov—"

Remy cut himself off in midsentence as he heard a familiar voice coming from the TV.

"This is about your cooking," the voice began.

"Hey! That's Gusteau!" Remy said excitedly to his brother. "Emile, look!"

The two brothers stared at the screen. "Great cooking is not for the faint of heart," explained

Gusteau. "You must be imaginative, strong-hearted. You must try things that may not work. And you must not let anyone . . ."

Remy walked toward the TV, completely transfixed.

". . . define your limits because of where you come from. Your only limit is your soul. What I say is true: anyone can cook." He looked at the camera sternly, then cracked a smile. "But only the fearless can be great."

"Pure poetry," Remy said in awe.

"But it was not to last," said the narrator on TV. "Gusteau's restaurant lost one of its five stars after a scathing review by France's top food critic, Anton Ego. It was a severe blow to Gusteau, and the great chef died shortly afterward—some say of a broken heart."

Remy was stunned. "Gusteau . . . is dead," he said in disbelief.

Suddenly, the TV clicked off. In the reflection of the screen, Remy could see that the old woman was awake and staring right at him.

*"Aah!"* shouted Remy. He sprinted past Emile, who was sitting in a dirty pan on the stove, stuffing his face with scraps.

The old woman reached into her umbrella stand and pulled out a shotgun. She aimed, and—*pop!*—an umbrella stuck in the end of the gun flew open. She tossed it aside, aimed again, and fired, narrowly missing the brothers.

"Run! Run! *Aah!*" yelled Remy.

Emile scrambled up the stovepipe as fast as his little legs could carry him. On autopilot, he ran toward the hole in the ceiling that led to the attic.

*"No!"* shouted Remy. "You'll lead her to the colony!"

The old woman blasted huge holes in the ceiling, just behind the scrambling Emile. He leapt clear of a blast—and landed on the end of a hanging light fixture. She leveled the gun barrel at the helplessly dangling Emile.

Remy hid his eyes. He couldn't watch.

The old woman aimed and fired. *Click*. The shotgun was empty. She raced off for more shells.

Emile struggled to pull his chubby body up into the light fixture. Remy ran to help his brother.

The old woman found a fresh box of shotgun shells, spilling them in her excitement. Emile swung the lamp back and forth until he was finally able to grab Remy's paw. *Yes!* But then the lamp swung backward, pulling Remy onto it, too.

As the woman loaded a shell into the shotgun, Remy and Emile scrambled up the lamp to the hole in the ceiling. She fired again. As the smoke cleared, she saw that she had missed both rats.

*Crack!* A chunk of ceiling broke free. Her last shot had completed a perfect circle of shotgun holes in the ceiling. All of a sudden, the attic floor, some furniture, and hundreds of very surprised rats came crashing down.

Not believing her eyes, the old woman screeched and ran out of the room.

Django hit the floor and started issuing orders.

"Evacuate! Sound the alarm!" he shouted.

The rats quickly began to stream out of the farmhouse. They were so intent on their flight that they barely registered the return of the old woman, who was now wearing a gas mask and wielding a gas canister.

In the yard, Remy and Emile fled along with the escaping mob of rats. Suddenly, to Emile's utter confusion, Remy stopped and turned back, battling upstream through the flood of fleeing rats. "The book!" he cried.

Inside, the old woman was madly spraying gas everywhere. Holding his breath, Remy summoned all his strength and pushed the cookbook across the counter and out the kitchen window.

At the riverbank, Django directed the panic-stricken rats to makeshift boats. The boats pushed off just as Remy, clutching Gusteau's cookbook, reached the shore. Using the book as a raft, Remy jumped on top of it and started paddling after the colony. "I'm coming!" he shouted.

"Hold on, Son!" called Django. He turned to the other rats. "Give him something to grab on to!"

The rats held out a spatula toward Remy.

"Paddle, Son!" Django shouted desperately.

Soon enough, Remy was able to get one paw onto the spatula and pull himself closer.

*Blam!* A shotgun blast hit the water, sending Remy flying off the book. Django looked up. The old woman was shooting from the footbridge directly above them.

"You can make it!" Django yelled hoarsely.

Remy struggled to get back onto the book and catch up with his family. As the old woman blasted away, the rat boats disappeared into a drainpipe. Remy climbed back onto the book and grabbed the spatula, using it as an oar. Before the old woman could reload and start firing again, Remy paddled into the drainpipe.

He was safe—for now.

Remy desperately tried to keep up with the other rats. But he was losing sight of them.

"Guys, wait! Stop!" he called.

"Paddle, Son!" shouted Django.

There was a sudden quiet, and then Remy heard a distant scream. What was going on?

"Dad?" he called. But the tunnel was silent.

Remy was alone. He hung his head and sighed. Then his eyes widened as he heard a deafening roar. He was headed toward an enormous waterfall! Remy started to paddle away from it as hard as he could, but the pull was too strong for the small rat. He screamed as he fell off the book and tumbled into the churning waters.

Finally, the waters calmed enough for him to climb back onto the cookbook. Remy was soaked to the bone, chilled, and exhausted.

After a while, he floated to a stop. He realized he was in the sewer. It was dark, cold, and stinky, but at least it was quiet and safe.

As the sun rose, light spilled through the sewer grate. Remy flipped through the pages of his beloved cookbook, trying to dry them. As he paused on a page of Gusteau showing off one of his creations, his stomach growled. Remy sighed.

And then, right before his unbelieving eyes, the photograph of the well-fed chef came to life!

"If you are hungry," Gusteau said, "go up and look around, Remy. Why do you wait and mope?"

"I've just lost my family," said Remy. "All my friends. Probably forever."

"How do you know?" the French chef asked.

"Well, I . . ." Remy stopped himself. "You are

an illustration. Why am I talking to you?"

The chef shrugged. "You just lost your family. All your friends. You are lonely."

"Yeah, well, you're dead," Remy retorted.

Gusteau smiled. "Ah . . . but that is no match for wishful thinking. If you focus on what you've left behind, you will never be able to see what lies ahead. Now, go up and look around."

Although Remy wasn't quite sure why, he took Gusteau's advice. He headed up the pipes and began to scurry through narrow spaces between the walls of buildings. He was terrifyingly close to the human world. Through a crack in the wall of one apartment, he spied a chunk of delicious-looking French bread. Nearly woozy with hunger, he grabbed it and prepared to take a bite.

"What are you doing?" Gusteau was back.

Remy was so startled he nearly dropped the bread. "I'm hungry. I don't know where I am, and I don't know when I'll find food again."

Gusteau shook his head. "Remy, you are better

than that. You are a cook! A cook makes. A thief takes. You are not a thief."

Remy put the bread back. "But I *am* hungry," he said.

Gusteau laughed. "Food will come, Remy. Food always comes to those who love to cook." Then he vanished again.

Remy shook his head. What a strange hallucination! He traveled up a pipe on the side of a building. Just when he thought he could go no farther, he emerged on a rooftop.

And what an amazing view awaited him! He blinked in disbelief as he took in the Paris skyline.

"Paris?" Remy said when he finally could speak. "All this time I've been underneath *Paris*? Wow! It's beautiful!"

"The *most* beautiful," said a voice. Remy spun around. Gusteau had returned.

Remy spotted the Eiffel Tower and Notre Dame, and then his eye lit on a landmark even more alluring—Gusteau's restaurant, only blocks away.

"Gusteau's?" said Remy in a reverent voice. "You've led me to your restaurant."

"It seems as though I have," replied Gusteau. "Yes. There it is! I have led you to it!"

"I gotta see this!" Remy cried, taking off toward the restaurant. Gusteau followed him.

In the kitchen of Gusteau's, several of the cooks were preparing for the dinner rush. Horst, Lalo, Larousse, and Colette were busy making soups, salads, soufflés, and other tasty dishes.

A small unpleasant-looking man in a tall chef's hat walked in. It was Skinner, the head chef.

"Hey, boss!" said Larousse excitedly. "Look who's here! This is Linguini, Renata's little boy."

Linguini, a thin, nervous-looking young man, stood up, knocking over his chair.

"All grown up, eh?" said Larousse. "You remember Renata, Gusteau's old flame?" he asked Skinner.

It was obvious that Skinner had no idea who

Larousse was talking about. "Ah, yes," he said. "So nice of you to visit. How is . . . ?"

"My mother?" asked Linguini. "Good. Well, not—she's been better—I mean, uh . . ." He trailed off uncomfortably.

"She died," finished Horst.

"Oh, I'm sorry," said Skinner.

"Don't be," said Linguini. "She believed in heaven, so she's covered. You know, afterlife-wise," he added awkwardly. Then he handed Skinner a sealed envelope.

"What's this?" asked Skinner.

"She left it for you," Linguini explained. "I think she hoped it would help. Me. You know, get a job. Here."

"But of course," Larousse said. "Gusteau wouldn't hesitate. Any son of Renata's is more than—"

Skinner cut him off. "Yes, well, we could file this, and if something suitable opens up . . ."

"We've already hired him," Larousse said.

"What?" spluttered Skinner. "How dare you hire someone without my permission!"

"We needed a garbage boy," Horst explained.

Skinner calmed down. "Oh, garbage. Well." He gave Linguini a thin, insincere smile. "I'm glad it worked out."

As Horst handed Linguini a hat and a uniform, Linguini gulped. What had he gotten himself into?

While all this was going on, Remy and Gusteau lay sprawled out on top of a skylight that looked down into the kitchen.

"I can't believe it," Remy said with a sigh. "A real gourmet kitchen, and I get to watch."

Gusteau chuckled. "You've read my book. Let us see how much you know, eh? Which one is the chef?"

Remy pointed to Skinner. "That guy."

"Very good. Who is next in command?"

"The sous-chef," said Remy, pointing to Horst. "The sous is responsible for the kitchen when the chef's not around."

"Hmm," said Gusteau approvingly.

Remy continued identifying the kitchen staff, excited to show off his knowledge. Gusteau was impressed. "You are a clever rat. Now, who is that?" He pointed to Linguini, the brand-new garbage boy, who was furiously scrubbing a pan.

"He's nobody," Remy said dismissively.

"Not nobody," said Gusteau, correcting him. "He is part of the kitchen."

"He's a *plongeur* or something," Remy said. "He washes dishes or takes out the garbage. He doesn't cook."

"But he could," said Gusteau.

Remy looked at Gusteau and chuckled. As if!

Just then, Linguini accidentally knocked over a pot of soup bubbling on the stove and spilled it onto the floor. Panicking, he quickly replaced the pot on the burner and mopped up the mess.

"How do you know?" asked Gusteau. "What do I always say? 'Anyone can cook.'"

Remy rolled his eyes. "Well, yeah. Anyone

*can*. That doesn't mean anyone *should*."

"Well, that is not stopping him," said Gusteau, pointing to Linguini. "See?"

Remy watched in horror as Linguini scooped some water from another pot and put it into the soup pot. Then Linguini began throwing in some random spices and vegetables. "What is he doing?" Remy gasped. "No! This is terrible! He can't—he's ruining the soup! And nobody's noticing!" He turned to Gusteau. "It's *your* restaurant! Do something!"

Gusteau shrugged. "What can I do? I am a figment of your imagination."

"But he's ruining the soup!" Remy shouted. "We've got to tell someone that he's—"

The skylight panel suddenly gave way under Remy's weight. He fell into the kitchen.

*Oh, no,* thought Remy as he fell. *Out of the frying pan and into the—*

*Splash!*

Luckily, Remy had landed in a sink filled with dishwater, not a pot of boiling water. Gasping for breath, he paddled to the surface and pulled himself out of the soapy mess.

Remy slipped over the edge of the counter and scrambled underneath it. He watched warily as the cooks' clog-clad feet marched by on each side. He gulped. He was surrounded by humans—the enemies of his kind.

The kitchen was loud, busy, and scary. Panicking, Remy ran out from under the counter, and someone almost stepped on him.

The refrigerator door swung open, knocking Remy across the floor and under the stove mid-bolt. Catching his breath, he peered out and noticed an open window across the kitchen. *Yes*—a way out!

Above him, rows of burners fired up. Remy raced across the walkway and slipped under another counter and to the other side, where he was nearly hit by a passing serving trolley.

Scurrying underneath the trolley, he made his way across the room. He finally reached a dish rack, which he used to climb onto the counter.

There it was—the open window, his means of escape. Remy ran toward it, scrambling over a covered pot. The lid of the pot slipped, and Remy fell inside. Then a chef picked up the pot and carried it back across the room! When he set it down, Remy jumped out and once again headed toward the window. But a tantalizing scent caught his attention. Even though all he wanted was to escape, there was nothing he could do in the thrall of such a wonderful aroma. He followed the scent to a pan filled with vegetables. He had just crawled into the pan when one of the chefs picked it up and slid it into the oven!

Flames ignited all around him as the oven was turned on.

Remy leapt out of the pan and escaped just as the chef was closing the oven door.

But Remy was still not safe. His death-defying jump had landed him on the lower shelf of a trolley, and he realized he was on his way into the dining room! A waiter named Mustafa reached onto the cart for a dish and grabbed Remy instead. *"Aah!"* the surprised waiter cried. Just then, another trolley rolled by, and Remy wriggled out of Mustafa's hands and jumped onto it.

Back in the kitchen, Remy scampered under a counter. He needed to get out—and fast! And that was just when one of the chefs reached over and closed the window.

Remy's heart sank. What was he going to do?

Linguini walked to the stove and tasted the soup he had doctored. *Ugh!* It tasted so horrible that Linguini ran over to the very same window, opened it, and spit out the soup. It was that bad.

Here was Remy's chance. He scurried to a broom leaning by the window, climbed it, and began to make his way across a shelf of spices that sat above the stove. Dodging the jars, he ran through the steam from the soup bubbling directly below. Remy winced. The smell was bad enough to peel the paint off the walls.

Remy paused. He didn't know what to do. Part of him wanted to stay—despite the danger—and save the soup. But the other part wanted to save himself! He glanced around the kitchen. The chefs hadn't noticed one indecisive rat. He looked again at the window—at freedom.

Suddenly, Gusteau appeared. "Remy!" he said urgently. "What are you waiting for? You know how to fix it. This is your chance."

Gusteau was right. This *was* his chance! Filled

with purpose, Remy jumped to the stove top, turned the burner down, then hopped up to the faucet to add water to the soup. He washed his hands and proceeded to remake the soup. He tasted, he sniffed. He salted, he peppered. He added vegetables and spices.

Remy took a big taste. "Ahhh." It was almost there. He grabbed another pawful of spices to add, and suddenly realized that Linguini was staring at him, his eyes wide with disbelief. They stared at each other, motionless.

Remy finally dropped the spices into the soup.

Just then, Skinner yelled, "The soup! Where is the soup?"

The two jumped. Remy tried to run for the window, but a quick-thinking Linguini slammed a colander over him. Remy was hidden. But he was also trapped.

"Out of my way!" yelled Skinner. "Move it, garbage boy!" He spotted a ladle in Linguini's hand. "You are cooking?" he thundered. He grabbed the terrified young man by the collar. "How dare you cook in my kitchen? Where do you get the gall to even attempt something so monumentally idiotic?" Skinner turned bright red. "I should have you drawn and quartered! I'll do it! I think the law is on my side!"

In all the excitement, Mustafa ladled out a bowl of the soup and brought it into the dining room.

It was too late by the time Skinner realized what was going on. "Sooooup!" he yelled. *"Stop that soup!"* He raced after Mustafa, but the soup was already being served. "Nooooo!"

Skinner dragged a stepladder to the dining room door and peered out the window. Then he turned around and glared at Linguini. "Linguini! You're fired! F-I-R-E-D! *FIRED!*"

Mustafa stuck his head through the double door and spoke in a low voice to Skinner.

"She wants to see the chef," he said.

The color drained from Skinner's face. He took

a deep breath and headed into the dining room. Moments later, he stalked back into the kitchen, a bewildered look on his face. Mustafa was right behind him.

"What did the customer say?" asked Colette.

"It was not a customer," explained Mustafa. "It was a critic."

Colette winced. "Ego?" she asked nervously.

Skinner was dazed. "Solene LeClaire," he said.

"LeClaire? What did she say?" asked Colette.

"She liked the soup," said Mustafa. He was mystified.

Skinner could not believe his ears. He rushed to the soup and tasted it. From the look on his face, it was clear that the soup was delicious—and that Skinner was not very happy about that.

The bustle of the kitchen stopped dead. Everyone stared at Skinner.

"What are you playing at?" Skinner asked Linguini suspiciously.

"I . . . uh . . . am I still fired?" asked Linguini.

"You can't fire him," argued Colette.

Skinner wheeled around. "What?"

Colette gathered up her courage and faced the angry chef. "LeClaire likes it, yeah? She made a point of telling you so. If she writes a review to that effect and finds out you fired the cook responsible—"

Skinner laughed dismissively. "He's a *garbage boy,*" he said with a sneer.

"Who made something she liked," Colette finished. "How can we claim to represent the name of Gusteau if we don't uphold his most cherished belief?"

"And what belief is that, Mademoiselle Tatou?" asked Skinner angrily.

"Anyone can cook," she said simply.

The staff looked at Skinner expectantly. "Perhaps I have been a bit harsh on our new garbage boy," he said in an icy voice. "He has taken a bold risk, and we should reward that as Chef Gusteau would have. If he wishes to swim in dangerous waters, who are we to deny him?"

Skinner turned to Colette. "Since you have expressed such an interest in his cooking career, you should be responsible for it," he said.

Colette's face fell.

"Anyone else?" said Skinner.

The other cooks quickly turned away, returning to their chopping and sautéing. Skinner gave Colette a withering smile. "Then back to work!"

While everyone's attention was elsewhere, Skinner turned to Linguini and spoke to him angrily under his breath. "You are either very lucky or very *un*lucky," he said. "You will make the soup again, and this time I'll be paying attention. Very close attention."

Linguini gulped.

Meanwhile, Remy was trying to make his escape. The colander kept moving, slowly but surely, toward the window. When Remy was close enough, he crawled out from underneath the colander, headed for freedom.

"They think you might be a cook," Skinner continued. "But you know what I think, Linguini? I think you are a sneaky, overreaching little—" From the corner of his eye, he spotted Remy.

*"Raaaaaat!"*

"A rat!" shouted Horst.

"Get the rat!" screamed Lalo.

Remy took off. Skinner grabbed a mop and swung at Remy, shattering dishes and blocking his escape.

"Linguini!" shouted Skinner. "Get something to trap it!"

Linguini grabbed a jar and forced Remy into it, then screwed the lid tightly shut.

"What should I do now?" he asked.

"Kill it," said Skinner.

"Now?" asked Linguini, looking around the kitchen.

"No! Not in the kitchen. Are you mad? Do you know what would happen to us if anyone knew we had a *rat* in our kitchen? They'd close us down!" Skinner took a breath and continued. "Our reputation is hanging by a thread as it is. Take it away from here—far away. Kill it, dispose of it. Go!"

Shaking, Linguini ran out the back door and hopped onto his bicycle. He began to pedal furiously into the gloom, almost hitting a parked car. He rode until he reached the bank of the Seine, the river that divides Paris. Linguini usually loved strolling the riverfront, so beautiful and serene. But that night, it looked dark and foreboding. He shivered. Linguini slowed his bicycle and pulled up by a streetlamp near the underpass of a bridge. He climbed off his bicycle, opened the jar, and held it over the water.

Remy was petrified.

"Don't look at me like that!" shouted Linguini. "You aren't the only one who's trapped. They expect me to cook it again!" He took a deep breath. "I mean, I'm not ambitious. I wasn't trying to cook. I was just trying to stay out of trouble. You're the one who was getting fancy with the spices!

"What did you throw in there?" he asked. "Oregano?"

Remy shook his head.

"No? What, rosemary?" asked Linguini.

Again Remy shook his head.

"That's a spice, isn't it? Rosemary?"

Remy nodded. Rosemary was indeed a spice.

"Then what was all the flipping and all the throwing the . . ." Linguini trailed off, frowned, and turned from Remy. He slumped down on the bank, setting the jar with Remy inside next to him. "I need this job," he explained. "I've lost so many. I don't know how to cook, and now I'm actually talking to a rat as if you—" He shook his head, suddenly realizing what was going on. "Huh? Did you *nod*? Have you been nodding?"

Remy nodded.

"You understand me?"

Remy nodded again.

"So I'm not crazy!" Linguini shouted.

Remy shook his head.

"Wait a second, wait a second—I can't cook." He turned to Remy for confirmation. "Can I?"

Remy shook his head once more. Linguini certainly could not cook; that was a fact.

"But you—you can, right?"

Remy hesitated. He didn't like to brag.

"Look, don't be so modest. You're a rat, for goodness' sake! Whatever you did, they liked it." He thought for a moment. "Yeah, this could work. Hey, they liked the soup. . . ." In his excitement, Linguini turned to Remy and accidentally knocked the jar into the Seine. Horrified, Linguini dove in after it.

Moments later, both Linguini and the jar were sitting on the riverbank again. Linguini was soaking wet, but he didn't miss a beat. "They liked the soup. Do you think you could . . . do it again?"

Remy nodded.

"Okay, I'm gonna let you out now," Linguini said. "But we're together on this right?"

Remy nodded again.

"Okay."

Linguini unscrewed the jar. And quick as a wink, Remy took off into the darkness. He cackled as he ran. He was free. *Sucker!* He thought of the hapless Linguini.

But something made him turn back. He saw Linguini standing forlornly under the bridge. Remy slowed to a stop and sighed.

Linguini sighed, too, and sadly walked to his bicycle. But then he heard a small noise and turned. Could it be? Yes! It was Remy, cautiously coming back toward him.

Linguini fumbled with the keys as he unlocked his apartment door. The warped door swung open, then caught. Linguini stepped inside and turned on a light, revealing a small, shabby, oddly shaped room. There were two mismatched chairs, a lone window, a tiny table with a hot plate, and a small ancient refrigerator. Perched on the arm of the ragged couch (which also served as the bed) was a small black-and-white television.

"So, this is it," Linguini told Remy. "I mean, it's not much, but it's, you know . . ." He looked around. "Not much," he finished lamely. "Could be worse. There's heat and light and a couch with a TV," he said with a shrug. "So, you know, what's mine is yours."

Remy checked out his new digs. Then he turned to Linguini with a big smile. He was delighted!

Later that night, an old French movie flickered on the TV as Linguini snored on the couch. Remy, tucked into an oven mitt on the windowsill, gazed dreamily at the lights of Paris. He grinned and closed his eyes. This was the beginning of his brand-new life.

# Chapter 6

The next morning, Linguini awoke with a start. He looked over at the windowsill.

"Morning, Little Chef," he said with a yawn. "Rise and shine." But the oven mitt was empty.

Linguini immediately assumed the worst. "Idiot!" he moaned at himself. "I knew this would happen! I let a rat into my place and tell him what's mine is his."

He rushed to the refrigerator, yanked it open, and looked inside. It was empty.

"Eggs gone! Stupid! He's stolen food and hit the road!" Linguini shook his head in disbelief at his own gullibility and foolishness. "What did I expect? That's what I get for trusting a ra—"

Linguini turned and discovered that Remy was cooking breakfast on the hot plate. The little rat looked quite pleased with himself. The table was set for two.

Linguini blinked. "What—is that for me?"

Remy nodded. Skillfully, but with effort, he spooned most of the eggs onto Linguini's plate and the rest onto his own. Linguini sat at the table and put a forkful into his mouth.

"Mmm. It's good," said Linguini. Then he glanced at his watch. "Oh, no! We're gonna be late! And on the first day! Come on, Little Chef!"

Linguini shoveled the rest of the eggs into his mouth and grabbed his coat. He picked up Remy and jammed him into his coat pocket before the hungry rat could get even a single forkful of eggs into his mouth. Then he ran out the door.

In Gusteau's kitchen, the cooks were all clustered around Colette as she read aloud a review from that morning's paper. Even Skinner was curious. He walked in and paused to listen.

"'Though I,'" read Colette, "'like many other critics, had written off Gusteau's since the great chef's death, the soup was a revelation, a spicy yet subtle taste experience.'"

Skinner was stunned. "Solene LeClaire?"

"Yes!" said Colette. She resumed reading. "'Against all odds, Gusteau's has recaptured our attention. Only time will tell if they deserve it.'"

Linguini had arrived at Gusteau's and now stood outside uncertainly. He held Remy in his palm as he frantically tried to figure out where to hide him. Under his shirt? No. Up his sleeve? Negative. In his sock? Impossible. Down his pants? Remy looked at him, appalled.

"Look, I know it's stupid and weird," Linguini said, desperation creeping into his voice. "But neither of us can do this alone. So we have to do this together. Right? You with me?"

Reluctantly, Remy nodded.

Linguini placed Remy inside his shirt. "So let's

do this thing!" he shouted, trying to psych himself up. With a burst of nervous energy, he slammed open the kitchen door and strode to his station. But having a rat in his clothing transformed Linguini's confident swagger into a strangely spastic lurch. The cooks watched their new coworker in silent amusement.

A tall white chef's hat—Linguini's new hat—rested at his station. Linguini picked it up, swallowed hard, and put it on his head.

All of a sudden, Skinner was beside him. Linguini jumped. "Now," Skinner said with a scowl, "re-create the soup." He smiled—a nasty smile. "Take as much time as you need." And with that, he stalked off.

Linguini looked down at his station.

"Soup," he said weakly.

So Linguini started to cook—or started *trying* to cook, to be more accurate. With no skill, no grace, and certainly no thought about what he was doing, he dumped the same ingredients he had used the day before into the pot and stirred.

Peeking out from Linguini's collar, Remy watched him at work. He had to stop him! Remy scrambled under Linguini's shirt and across his chest. Linguini couldn't help giggling. That tickled!

Remy's head next popped out from Linguini's shirt cuff. He inhaled the aroma from the bubbling soup—and gagged. Good—Linguini was reaching for a spice! Bad—it was the wrong spice! Remy raced back across Linguini's chest to the opposite sleeve and gave Linguini's hand a sharp bite. Linguini yelped and dropped the spice tin.

Remy scurried to the other arm, causing Linguini to giggle again. He gave Linguini yet another nip, and Linguini angrily smacked him.

The other cooks were dumbfounded as they watched Linguini's strange movements.

Finally, Linguini couldn't take it any longer. He lurched across the kitchen floor and into the refrigerated food safe, closing the door behind him. He ripped his shirt open, revealing his chest and arms, which were covered in red bite marks. *"Aaaahh!"* he screamed. "This is not going to work, Little Chef. I am going to lose it if we do this anymore. We've got to figure out something else. Something that doesn't involve biting or nipping or running up and down my body with your little rat feet."

But Remy could barely listen. He was busy staring at all the wonderful food around him. He hadn't eaten all morning, and he was famished.

"Little Chef?" Linguini said quizzically. Then he realized what was going on. "You're hungry!" He looked at Remy. He knew he shouldn't take food from the safe, but his tiny friend needed to eat. He quickly broke off a chunk of cheese for Remy, who gobbled it down gratefully.

"Okay," began Linguini, calmer now. "Let's think this out. You know how to cook. And I know how to"—he paused for a moment—"appear human. We just need to work out a system so that I do what you want in a way that doesn't look like

I'm being controlled by a tiny rat chef." He paused as the reality of what he had just said sank in. "Oh, would you listen to me? I'm insane. I'm insane. I'm inside a refrigerator, talking to a rat about gourmet cooking. I will never pull this off."

Curious, Skinner paused outside the door to listen. Realizing that Linguini was in his precious food safe, he threw the door open.

Quick as a wink, Linguini's hand shot out and flipped the light switch. But not before Skinner caught a glimpse of something—something very odd. Had he just seen Linguini talking to a *rat*? Skinner threw the light back on. And there was Linguini. But he was alone.

"The rat! I saw it!" Skinner shouted.

"A rat?" Linguini asked innocently.

"Yes, yes!" Skinner answered. "A rat. Right next to you." He thought for a moment. "What are you doing in here?" he asked suspiciously.

"I'm just familiarizing myself with, you know . . ." Linguini glanced wildly around the food safe. “The vegetables. And such.”

Skinner’s eyes narrowed. He knew that this garbage boy was up to no good. “Get out,” he said.

Linguini returned to the kitchen.

So, where was Remy? When the lights had gone out, Linguini had quickly shoved the rat the only place he could think of—under his high white hat. Linguini whispered to the top of his head, “That was close. You okay up there?”

Remy nodded. Then he looked up to see that Linguini was about to collide with Mustafa, who was carrying a tray loaded high with dishes. This was going to be a disaster of epic proportions! Without thinking, Remy grabbed two handfuls of Linguini’s hair and yanked on them as on a horse’s reins. Linguini jerked backward so far under the tray of dishes, it looked like he was doing the limbo. Crisis averted!

Linguini blinked in amazement and ducked into the bathroom. He stood in front of the mirror and removed his hat so that he could address

Remy directly. "How did you do that?" he asked.

Remy shrugged. He didn't have a clue. He looked down at his paws, still grasping tufts of Linguini's hair. Experimentally, Remy gave the left tuft a big jerk. Linguini's left arm shot up.

"Whoa!" exclaimed Linguini.

Remy tugged again, and Linguini's leg suddenly kicked out. A wild gleam came into Remy's eyes. Like a child with a new toy, he gleefully began yanking tufts from various parts of Linguini's head. Linguini jerked around the bathroom like an out-of-control marionette.

"Whoa!" Linguini cried. "That's strangely involuntary." He fell down onto the toilet seat.

Remy stopped pulling.

The two friends looked at each other. They had the same crazy idea.

Later that night, in Linguini's tiny apartment, it was time for some more experimenting. Linguini placed a cutting board and several utensils on the kitchen counter. "Okay," he said. Remy gestured that Linguini should blindfold himself. Then, from his perch on top of Linguini's head, Remy began pulling his hair, directing him around the kitchen.

After much trial and error—several near falls, a close call with a cactus, the accidental launch of a frying pan out the window, and some flying pasta—Remy and Linguini moved on to pouring.

The first try was a disaster. Red wine spilled all over the kitchen counter. Finally, Linguini was able to center the bottle over the glass. He barely breathed as he poured, spilling not a drop. He smiled and raised his glass in a toast.

Next he lifted the glass to Remy, who prepared to sip. But Linguini tipped the glass too far and poured wine all over Remy.

Their practice eventually began to pay off. Remy successfully directed Linguini as he chopped an onion and cracked an egg. Within a few hours, the two of them were working together like a well-oiled machine.

# Chapter 7

The next morning, Linguini, with Remy hidden inside his chef's hat, chopped and seasoned, seasoned and chopped. He was making the soup—Remy's way.

When they were done, Skinner came to taste it. Linguini nervously hovered nearby.

"Congratulations," Skinner said in a surly tone. "You were able to repeat your accidental success. But you will need to know more than soup if you are to survive in my kitchen, boy."

At her station, Colette scowled. She knew for certain what was coming next. "Colette will be responsible for teaching you how we do things here," Skinner finished with an evil grin.

As Skinner stalked away, Linguini turned to the pretty young chef with a big smile.

"Listen," he began, "I just want you to know how honored I am to be studying under such a . . ." He trailed off, noticing the knives she was holding. *"Aah!"*

Colette stabbed the knives one by one through Linguini's shirtsleeve, pinning it to the table. She was the only woman in the kitchen, she explained, because haute cuisine was considered a man's world, so she had to be the toughest cook.

"I have worked too hard for too long to get here, and I'm not going to jeopardize it for some garbage boy who got lucky," she said. "Got it?"

Linguini nodded pathetically.

Colette grabbed the knife handles with one hand and pulled them out with a single jerk. Linguini toppled to the ground. He pulled himself up and watched as Colette stomped off. She was scary. Scary—but impressive.

Sitting in his office, Skinner noticed the unopened letter from Linguini's mother lying on his desk. He opened the envelope and began to read. His eyes grew wide with alarm. He immediately called his lawyer.

An hour later, Skinner paced back and forth in his office as his lawyer, Talon Labarthe, took another look at Gusteau's last will and testament.

Talon cleared his throat. "Well, this will stipulates that if after a period of two years from the date of death no heir appears, Gusteau's business interests will pass to his sous-chef. You."

"I *know* what the will stipulates!" Skinner said angrily. "What I want to know is if this letter"—he held it aloft—"if this *boy* changes anything!"

Skinner raised the blinds to reveal Linguini. Next to the practiced cooking staff, Linguini looked even more awkward than usual.

"He's not Gusteau's son!" Skinner thundered.

"Gusteau had no children! And what of the timing of all of this? The deadline for the will expires in less than a month!" He narrowed his eyes. "Suddenly some boy arrives with a letter from his 'recently deceased' mother claiming Gusteau as his father? Highly suspect!"

Talon noticed Gusteau's chef's hat in a display case. He began to study it closely.

"But the boy does not know?" he asked.

Skinner brandished the letter. "His mother claimed she never told him—or Gusteau. And asks that I not tell!"

"Why you?" asked Talon. "What does she want?" He spotted a hair on Gusteau's hat. He pulled a pair of tweezers from his coat and removed the hair, then folded it carefully inside a handkerchief and placed it in his breast pocket.

"A job," answered Skinner. "For the boy."

"Then what are you worried about?" said Talon. "If he works here, you'll be able to keep an eye on him while I do a little digging. Find out how much of this is real." He put on his coat. "I will need you to collect some DNA samples from the boy. Hair, maybe."

"Mark my words," said Skinner. Paranoia began to creep into his voice. "The whole thing is highly suspect. He knows something!"

"Relax," said the lawyer as he opened the office door. "He's a garbage boy. I think you can handle this."

Colette might not have been happy with her new role as Linguini's tutor, but she grudgingly began to help him out.

Step by step, both Remy and Linguini began to learn how to be part of a well-run kitchen. Colette taught Linguini how to chop quickly and efficiently; how to keep his messy workstation clear so that things wouldn't slow down; and how to minimize cuts, burns, and spills—and keep his sleeves clean—by keeping his hands and arms close to his body at all times. And then there was

Remy's favorite lesson: how to identify a good bread by the pleasing crunch of its crust.

With his neat sleeves, superior chopping technique, and clean workstation, Linguini was finally an accepted member of the kitchen staff.

One night, Mustafa burst excitedly into the kitchen. "Someone has asked what is new!" he announced. "What do I tell them?"

"Hmmm," mused Skinner. "This is simple. Just pull out an old Gusteau recipe, something we haven't made in a while, and—"

"They know about the old stuff," interrupted Mustafa. "They like Linguini's soup."

Skinner's mouth fell open. "They are asking for food from Linguini?" An idea came to Skinner—an evil idea. He almost rubbed his hands together in anticipation. "Very well," he said. "If it's Linguini they want"—he spoke low so that only Mustafa could hear—"tell them Chef Linguini has prepared something special for them,

Remy and Gusteau watch the chefs from the skylight above the restaurant kitchen.

Remy is scared when he first arrives in the kitchen at Gusteau's.

Remy can't resist fixing the soup before he leaves.

Oh, no! Linguini, the garbage boy, catches Remy cooking.

Skinner, the head chef, is not pleased
with Linguini.

Linguini is nervous as Skinner orders
him to get rid of the rat.

Linguini realizes that the little rat might be able to help him in the kitchen.

Remy cooks a delicious breakfast for his new friend, Linguini.

With Remy under his hat, Linguini gets some helpful cooking tips from Colette.

Skinner tastes the soup that Linguini (and Remy) made. It is delicious.

Emile enjoys the cheese his brother Remy gives him.

In the kitchen, Remy tries to control the still-sleeping Linguini.

Remy presents himself to the cooks as the chef. A rat?! In the kitchen?! The cooks quit in protest!

Django and Emile show up to help Remy make the most important meal of his life.

Ego, the most powerful food critic in Paris, can make or break a restaurant with a single review. What will he think of Remy's ratatouille?

something definitely off-menu. And don't forget to stress its Linguini-ness."

Mustafa nodded and left. Skinner closed in on Linguini, a nasty smile on his face. "Now is your chance to try something worthy of your talent, Linguini. A forgotten favorite of the Chef's—Sweetbread à la Gusteau! Colette will help you."

"*Oui*, Chef," said Colette.

"Now, hurry up!" Skinner demanded. "Our diners are hungry!"

As Skinner headed to his office, Larousse pulled him aside. "Are you sure?" he asked. He sounded concerned. "That recipe was a disaster. Gusteau himself said so."

Skinner grinned nastily. "Just the sort of challenge a budding chef needs," he said. He disappeared into his office, humming happily to himself. His evil plan had been set into motion.

Colette and Linguini stared at the old, yellowing recipe card.

"'Sweetbread à la Gusteau,'" Colette read. "'Sweetbread cooked in a seaweed-salt crust with . . . cuttlefish tentacle . . .'" Her voice faltered. "'Dog rose puree, gooey duck egg, *dried white fungus?* Anchovy-licorice sauce?'" She blinked and shrugged it off. Colette liked to follow recipes, especially Gusteau's.

"I don't know this recipe," she admitted to Linguini. "But it is Gusteau, so . . ." She turned. "Lalo!" she called out. "We have some veal stomach soaking, yes?"

"Yes! I get some!" he shouted back.

"Uh, veal stomach?" said Linguini queasily.

Soon Remy was piloting Linguini's hand to lift the small pot of sauce off the burner and up to Linguini's hat for Remy to sniff.

Remy started to direct Linguini to dump it into a larger pot, then hesitated. He had an idea.

They added some spices, then leaned in for a sniff. *Yum!* Remy liked what he smelled. He decided he needed to improvise some more. Yanking Linguini's hair, he piloted the chef away from his station. Linguini staggered past the other chefs' workstations, wildly looking for his next ingredient. The other chefs watched in shock as he grabbed ingredients, raced back to his station, and dumped them into his pan.

Colette looked up from her preparation. "What are you doing?" she asked. "We are supposed to be preparing the Gusteau recipe."

Linguini stirred the sauce. "This is the recipe."

Colette shook her head. "The recipe doesn't

call for white truffle oil! What else have you—" She peered into Linguini's pan.

"Improvising?" she asked, appalled. "This is no time to experiment. The customers are waiting!"

Linguini was not pleased with Remy. "You're right," he said. He whacked his hat. "I should listen to you." He whacked his hat again. Angry, Remy pulled Linguini's hair hard. Then he had Linguini slap himself right across the face. *"Ow!"* Linguini cried.

"Where is the special order?" asked Horst.

Both Colette and Linguini were working intently.

"Coming!" called Colette. She turned to Linguini. "I thought we were together on this," she said in a low voice.

"We *are* together," said Linguini.

"Then what are you doing?" asked Colette.

"It's *very* hard to explain," answered Linguini.

"The special?" asked Horst, losing patience.

"Come get it!" shouted Colette.

Under the hat, Remy watched Colette anxiously. She set down the plate to be picked up.

"I forgot to add the anchovy-licorice sauce!" she suddenly said.

As she rushed back to her station to get it, Remy saw his chance. Linguini, much to his own dismay, found himself grabbing his pan and hurtling past Colette.

Colette was just about to add her sauce when Linguini swooped in and blocked her hand. In front of her disbelieving eyes, he dropped his sauté onto her sweetbread the moment before it was swept away to the dining room.

"Sorry," Linguini said sheepishly.

Skinner walked up to Horst with a big smile on his face.

"Is Linguini's dish done yet?" he asked eagerly.

"Ya," said Horst matter-of-factly. "It's as bad as we remembered. Just went out."

Skinner smiled. "Did you taste it?"

"Yeah, of course," said Horst.

Skinner's smile grew wider.

"Before he changed it," finished Horst.

"Good," said Skinner. Then he realized what Horst had said. "What? How could he change it?" he shrieked.

"He changed it as it was going out the door," said Horst.

Speechless, Skinner headed toward the dining room door just as Mustafa burst through it, excited.

"They love it!" the waiter cried. "Other diners are already asking about it, about Linguini. I have seven more orders."

*Seven more orders!* Inside Linguini's hat, Remy could barely contain his glee.

*Seven more orders!* Skinner couldn't believe it. "That's . . ." He tried to force a pleasant smile, but the angry tics erupting on his face gave him away. "Wonderful," he spit out.

Later, when the dinner rush was over, the chefs toasted Linguini's success. Everyone seemed genuinely happy for him. Everyone, that is, except Colctte, who was still stinging from his last-minute substitution.

Skinner watched from across the kitchen. He felt confused and resentful. He knew that something strange was going on, but he just couldn't figure out what it was. He shook his head as he watched Linguini cross the room in front of a light and—wait. What was that strange shadow inside Linguini's hat? It looked almost *rat-shaped*!

Moments later, Linguini stepped outside, quickly looked around to make sure no one was watching, and took off his hat.

"Take a break, Little Chef," said Linguini. "Get some air. We really did it tonight."

Remy was completely exhausted but exhilarated by the evening's success. He beamed at Linguini, who raised his glass in a salute to Remy before heading back inside.

In the meantime, Skinner had climbed to the top of a shelf. He needed to be at hat level to unmask—or unhat—Linguini. As Linguini crossed in front of him, Skinner snatched the hat from his head, revealing . . . a bad case of hat hair but nothing else.

Skinner gasped in confusion. Then, not knowing what to do, he lamely tried to cover his strange behavior. "Got your hat!" he called, waving it at Linguini playfully. He hopped to the ground and handed it back to the mystified Linguini.

"Seriously, now," said Skinner, "I'd love to have a little talk with you, Linguini, in my office."

"Am I in trouble?" Linguini asked worriedly.

Skinner gave Linguini's back a reassuring pat as he steered the boy into his office. "Trouble? Nooooo. A friendly chat. Just us cooks."

Colette watched as Linguini headed into Skinner's office. The door closed behind them.

Horst sidled up to her. "The *plongeur* won't be coming to you for advice anymore, eh, Colette?"

he said with a chuckle. "He's gotten all he needs."

Colette sighed sadly. She grabbed her coat and left the restaurant.

Skinner decided on a new tactic to get to the bottom of things—direct interrogation. He settled in behind Gusteau's desk. Linguini sat uneasily in a chair facing him, holding his glass of wine.

"Toasting your success, eh, Linguini?" Skinner said jovially. "Good for you."

"Oh, I just took it to be polite," explained Linguini. "I don't really drink, you know—"

"Of course you don't!" agreed Skinner. "I wouldn't either if I was drinking *that*." He plucked the glass from Linguini's hand and poured the offending liquid into the wastebasket. Then he held up a newly decanted bottle of wine.

"But you would have to be an idiot of elephantine proportions not to appreciate this," Skinner continued. "And you, Monsieur Linguini, are no idiot." He poured a glass of rich red wine and handed it to Linguini. "Let us toast to your non-idiocy!" he cried.

They sipped. Skinner was right. Linguini didn't know much about wine, but he knew one thing: *this* was delicious!

At the back entrance of Gusteau's, Remy munched contentedly on his dinner and stared at the starry sky. Everything was simply perfect—the bread, with its perfectly crispy crust, the cheese, with its perfectly sharp and nutty flavor, and his perfectly perfect life.

He suddenly froze, startled by a rustling sound behind the garbage cans. His first instinct was to run, but he was also curious. He crept closer.

"Remy?" said a familiar voice.

"Emile?" cried Remy.

The two brothers rushed to embrace each other, laughing with joy.

"What are you doing here?" Remy asked. "I thought I'd never see you guys again! I thought that was it! What are the chances we would find each other?"

"I can't believe it!" Emile exclaimed. "You're alive! You made it! Everybody thought you were a goner! We figured you didn't survive the rapids!"

"And what are you eating?" Remy asked his brother suspiciously.

Emile held up a piece of unidentifiable trash and took a bite. "I don't really know," he admitted. "I think it was some sort of wrapper once."

Remy grabbed the garbage from Emile and tossed it away with a flourish.

"What?" Remy said. "No, you're in Paris now, baby. My town. No brother of mine eats rejectamenta in my town!"

Emile waited outside while Remy went into the kitchen to find him some food. Remy headed right for the food safe. Just as he was about to open it, he paused. At that moment, he heard Linguini laugh in Skinner's office. Remy felt a pang of guilt, but still he pushed the latch open, jumped to the ground, and walked in.

He found Gusteau inside.

"Remy," said Gusteau. "You are stealing? You told Linguini he could trust you!"

"And he can," said Remy. "It's for my brother."

"But the boy could lose his job," said Gusteau admonishingly.

"Which means I would, too. It's under control, okay?" Remy replied.

In Skinner's office, Linguini was looking more relaxed. In fact, he was looking rather tipsy.

"Tell me, Linguini, about your interests," said Skinner. "Do you like animals?"

Linguini laughed. "What—animals? What kind?"

"Oh, the usual," Skinner said. "Dogs, cats, horses, guinea pigs . . . *rats.*"

But Linguini just looked at him with a goofy grin.

Skinner sighed. This wasn't going to be easy!

Remy walked out of the kitchen with a bundle of fruits and cheeses for his brother. Emile, left to his own devices, had found some more garbage and was happily munching away.

"Hey, I brought you something to—" Remy gasped when he saw his brother. "No, no, no! Spit that out right now!"

Ever obliging, Emile spit out the garbage. He looked embarrassed.

Remy sighed. Would his brother ever understand what food was all about? He handed Emile the fine cheese and fruit.

Suddenly, Emile realized something. "Hey! What are we doing? Dad doesn't know you're alive yet. We've got to go to the colony! Everyone will be thrilled!"

*The colony?* Remy wasn't sure about that. "Yeah, but, uh—"

"What?" asked Emile.

"Thing is, I kind of have to . . . uh . . ." Remy gestured vaguely at the kitchen. Emile frowned.

"What do you *hafta* more than family?" he asked. "What's more important here?" Emile stared furiously at his brother. Remy gazed back, his resolve starting to crumble. Deep inside, he had known that his perfect new life was too good to last. He looked nervously toward the kitchen.

"Well, I—it wouldn't hurt to visit," said Remy.

By this time, Skinner had uncorked several bottles of his finest wine but had gotten nowhere in his interrogation.

"Have you ever had a pet rat?" asked the desperate Skinner.

"Nope," answered Linguini.

"Did you work in a lab with rats?" he asked.

"Nope."

"Perhaps you lived in squalor at some point?" he asked.

"Nopety nopety no."

Skinner had reached his limit. "You know something about rats!" he yelled.

"Ratta tatta—hey!" said Linguini nonsensically. "Why do they call it that?"

"What?" asked Skinner, annoyed.

"Ratatouille! It's like a stew, right?" Linguini asked. "Why do they call it that? If you're gonna name a food, you should give it a name that sounds delicious. Ratatouille doesn't sound delicious." He thought for a moment. "It sounds like rat. And patooty. Rat patooty. Which does not sound delicious!" he concluded.

Linguini raised his glass to his lips to take another sip. But alas, his glass was empty. He held it out for Skinner to refill.

Skinner scowled. "Regrettably," he said, dropping the empty bottle into the trash with a loud thunk, "we're all out."

# Chapter 9

Remy shuddered with disgust as Emile led him through the underground labyrinth of the Paris sewer system. It was dark, wet, dirty, and cold.

Soon they arrived at the new rat encampment. The rat clan was thrilled by Remy's return. But no one was quite as happy as Django. He clasped paws with his son and raised their arms into the air victoriously.

"My son has returned!" he shouted to the cheering rat crowd.

The festive spirit soon turned into an all-out party—a swingin' rat party with drinks, music, and dancing. Django, Remy, and Emile sat at the head table. They raised their thimble glasses in a toast to welcome Remy home.

Django turned to Remy. "Finding someone to replace you as poison checker has been a disaster," he said. "Nothing's been poisoned, thank goodness, but it hasn't been easy. . . . Well, the important thing is you're home."

Remy took a deep breath. "Yeah, well, about that—"

"It's tough out there in the big world, isn't it?" Django interrupted.

"It's not like I'm a kid anymore," Remy said. "I can take care of myself. I found a nice spot not far away, so I'll be able to visit often."

"Visit?" Django said. He couldn't have heard his son correctly. "What? You're not staying?"

"No. It's not a big deal, Dad," Remy said. "I just—you didn't think I was going to stay forever, did you?"

As Remy and Django continued arguing, Emile tried to ease the tension. "Hey, the band's really on tonight, huh?" he said. But Remy and Django just ignored him.

"Rats," Remy continued. "All we do is take, Dad. I'm tired of taking! I want to make things! I want to add something to this world."

"You're talking like a human," Django said.

"Who are not as bad as you say."

"Oh, yeah?" Django challenged. "What makes you so sure?"

"I've been able to observe them at a close-ish sort of range," Remy said carefully. "And they're, you know, not so bad. As you say. They are."

Django had an idea. "Come with me," he said to Remy. "There's something I want you to see."

Django and Remy walked in silence until they arrived at an exterminator's shop. Remy was horrified. The window was filled scary-looking rattraps. "The world we live in belongs to the enemy," Django said. "We must live carefully. We look out for our own kind, Remy. When all is said and done, we're all we've got."

“No,” Remy said angrily. “Dad, I don’t believe it. You’re telling me that the future is—can only be—more of this.” He pointed to the gruesome exterminator shop.

“This is the way things are,” Django said. “You can’t change nature.”

“Change *is* nature, Dad. The part that we can influence. And it starts when we decide.” And with that, Remy headed back toward Gusteau’s.

As the sun was coming up, a tired Remy emerged from the sewer grate. He took a deep, cleansing breath of the fresh Parisian air. He exhaled, happy to be back in his new world. Standing upright,he headed for the kitchen entrance.

He went into the restaurant and looked around. No one had arrived yet. Remy stepped out onto the countertop and surveyed the kitchen, savoring the possibilities ahead. Suddenly, a sound—an awful, gear-grinding, choking sound—made him jump. Cautiously, Remy crept forward.

He peered over the edge of the countertop—and there was Linguini, curled up on the floor, sound asleep. To make matters worse, Remy could hear Colette's motorcycle approaching.

Without a moment to lose, Remy jumped onto Linguini's head and grabbed a tuft of his hair in each tiny paw. Tugging them expertly, he managed to get Linguini to his feet and standing upright. But try as he might, he just couldn't wake him.

Frantically, he looked around the kitchen. What was he going to do? He spotted a pair of sunglasses. He slipped them over Linguini's eyes just as Colette walked through the back door.

Colette took a deep breath, crossed the room, and began to prep. Somehow, Remy was able to make Linguini chop his vegetables in a lazy but convincing way. But with his sunglasses and sleepy movements, Linguini had an annoying air of over-confidence about him.

"Morning," Colette said coldly.

Remy gasped. There was no way to make

Linguini talk. So he kept Linguini chopping away.

Colette was irritated. Was Linguini ignoring her? "Good morning," she repeated.

Not knowing what else to do, Remy turned Linguini's head. It swiveled toward Colette and gave her a nod. Colette continued to prep. "So. The chef. He invited you in for a drink? That's big. What did he say?" she asked.

In desperation, Remy turned Linguini's head again. Linguini faced Colette with a goofy smirk plastered across his face.

"What—what, you can't tell me? Oh, forgive me for intruding on your deep, personal relationship with the chef," Colette said, furious. She turned and began sharpening her knife angrily. "I see how it is. You get me to teach you a few kitchen tricks to dazzle the boss and then you blow past me?"

Under the hat, Remy was panicking. This could not be going any worse! He kept Linguini chopping, hoping desperately for a way to salvage the situation. He hopped up and down on Linguini's head. "Wake up, wake up!" he squeaked.

Colette was upset. "I thought you were different," she said. "I thought you thought I was different. I thought—"

Not wanting Linguini to ignore her, Remy swung Linguini's head toward Colette. Big mistake. First Linguini's smirking face lolled in her direction. And then he let out a loud snore.

Colette gasped, then reached over and slapped Linguini right across the face. Linguini spun around twice before crashing to the floor. *Now* he was awake! *And* completely confused. What was he doing on the kitchen floor? Why was he wearing sunglasses in the kitchen? Why was Colette standing over him, looking so angry? He stared up at her.

Colette spoke, holding back her tears. "I didn't have to help you," she said. "If I'd looked out only for myself, I would have let you drown. But . . ." She took a deep breath. "I wanted you to succeed.

I . . . liked you. My mistake." She turned on her heel and stormed out the back door.

"Colette!" Linguini cried. "Wait! Colette!"

He and Remy both watched her go. Linguini turned to Remy, who peered out of Linguini's fallen hat.

"It's over, Little Chef," he said softly. "I can't do it anymore."

Linguini grabbed the hat with Remy in it, put it back on his head, and ran after Colette.

He found her climbing onto her motorcycle, about to make a getaway.

"Colette! Wait, wait, wait! Don't motorcycle away. Look, I'm no good with words. I'm no good with food, either. At least, not without your help."

Colette rolled her eyes. "I hate false modesty. It's just another way to lie. You have talent."

"No, but I don't," said Linguini. "Really! It's not me!"

Remy was starting to get worried. "Don't do it," he whispered.

"I have a secret. It's sort of disturbing," Linguini said. "I have a rrr . . ."

"You have a rash?" she guessed.

"No! I have this tiny, little, little, gahhh!" He took a deep breath and started speaking very quickly. "A tiny chef who tells me what to do."

Colette stared at him as if he had two heads. "A . . . 'tiny chef'?" she repeated.

"Yes. He's . . . uh . . ." He pointed to his hat. "He's up here."

"In your brain," said Colette.

Linguini sighed in frustration. "Okay. Here we go. You . . . inspire me. I'm going to risk it all. I'm going to risk looking like the biggest idiot psycho you've ever seen."

Linguini stared at Colette intently. "I mean, you want to know why I'm such a fast learner? You want to know why I'm such a great cook? Don't laugh! I'm going to show you." He slowly raised his arms toward his head.

"No!" Remy gasped. Linguini was about to

ruin everything! Thinking fast, Remy yanked Linguini's hair. Linguini's head jerked forward, and without warning, he planted a big kiss on Colette's lips.

Teeth gritted, concentrating heavily, Remy held on to Linguini's hair and kept the kiss going. He had no idea how they were going to react.

As Linguini and Colette continued to kiss, their eyes betrayed a myriad of emotions—first surprise, then fear, anger, and vulnerability, and finally happiness. They wrapped their arms around each other.

Remy collapsed on top of Linguini's head, breathing a sigh of relief. His secret was still safe—for now.

# Chapter 10

For a man who ate food for a living, Anton Ego was incredibly thin. Some might even have described him as cadaverous. He sat in his antique-filled office, poised over an ancient typewriter. The door opened, and his assistant, Ambrister Minion, entered.

"What is it, Ambrister?" Ego asked.

"Gusteau's," Minion said. "It's come back. It's popular."

"I haven't reviewed Gusteau's in years," Ego said in disbelief.

"No, sir," said Minion.

Ego pulled open his files and deftly flipped

through the folders. "My last review condemned it to the tourist trade," he said.

"Yes, sir," said Minion.

Ego pulled out the review and began to read. "I said, 'Gusteau has finally found his rightful place in history, right alongside an equally famous chef, Monsieur Boyardee.'"

"Touché," said Minion.

Rising from his desk, Ego moved menacingly toward Minion.

"That is where I left it. *That* was my last word. *The* last word."

"Yes," said Minion.

"Then tell me, Ambrister," said Ego, leaning toward his assistant. "How could it be popular?"

Back at Gusteau's, Skinner had just gotten some bad news from his lawyer—some very bad news.

"No. No. NO!" he groaned.

"The DNA matches," said Talon, calmly sipping a strong espresso. "The timing works;

everything checks out. He is Gusteau's son."

"This can't just happen!" whined Skinner. "The whole thing is a setup! The boy knows!" He walked to his office window and stared out at the bumbling Linguini. "Look at him out there, pretending to be an idiot. He's toying with my mind, like a cat with a ball of . . . something!"

"String?" suggested Talon.

"Yes!" cried Skinner. "Playing dumb! Taunting me with that rat!"

"Rat?" asked Talon.

Skinner went on and on with his rat theory: the rat was part of a plot Linguini had hatched to make Skinner think he was crazy. Apparently, it was working.

"The deadline passes in three days," said Talon, closing his briefcase. "Then you can fire him whenever he ceases to be valuable, and no one will ever know." He pulled on his coat, then paused at the door.

"I worried about the hair samples you gave

me. I had to send them back to the lab."

"Why?" asked Skinner.

"Because the first time they came back identified as rodent hair," Talon said with a shrug.

*Rodent* hair? Skinner nearly fell over.

The kiss might have saved Remy momentarily, but now he was paying for it. Linguini was officially head over heels for Colette, and Remy suddenly had no control over him. No amount of hair tugs could get Linguini to do his bidding. In the middle of a recipe, Remy had Linguini grab a certain spice he needed.

"No, no, no," Colette said, handing him a different one. "Try this. It's better."

Linguini smiled and reached for it. Horrified, Remy pulled his hair, trying to keep control, but *Linguini overrode Remy's command and took the spice!*

The next morning, Remy made his way down the

alley toward Gusteau's. There he discovered his brother and a bunch of his friends. They were hungry and looking for food. Remy was angry. But then he softened. He'd get them food. But just this once.

Inside, he discovered that the food safe was locked. He'd have to find the key in Skinner's office. Remy was pretty sure he knew where the key was. After a lot of effort, he managed to open a desk drawer and began to rummage through its contents. Remy stared in disbelief—for the key was hidden under a file labeled GUSTEAU: LAST WILL AND TESTAMENT. Remy turned to the Gusteau portrait that hung in the office.

"Your will!" he exclaimed.

Remy pulled open the file and discovered its startling contents—Gusteau's will, recent press clippings about the restaurant featuring Linguini, and an envelope with Linguini's mother's return address in the corner.

"Mind if I . . . ?" he asked the portrait, indicating the letter.

"Not at all," Gusteau replied, his portrait suddenly coming to life.

"Linguini? Why would Linguini be filed with your will?" Remy asked.

"This used to be my office," Gusteau said.

Remy pulled the letter from the envelope and read it without saying a word. Then he read the will. Then he read the letter again, his eyes wide with amazement.

"He's your son?" Remy squeaked.

"I have a . . . son?" Gusteau was flabbergasted.

"How could you not know this?" asked Remy.

"I am a figment of your imagination!" argued Gusteau. "*You* did not know! How could I?"

"Well, your son is the rightful owner of this restaurant!" said Remy.

At that moment, Skinner walked into his office. He froze in his tracks, stunned by the bizarre sight of a rat sitting on his desk, reading his personal mail!

Remy snatched the letter and the will in his

mouth and made a run for it.

"No! No!" screamed Skinner. "The rat . . . it's—*aah!*"

Remy raced outside. Skinner burst out the back door and pushed Lalo, who had just arrived, off his scooter. Skinner jumped onto the moped and took off in hot pursuit. He and Remy dodged traffic, racing through the Parisian streets.

It was inevitable for a man on a scooter to outrun a small rodent. Skinner reached down to snatch the documents from Remy when the rat suddenly stopped. Skinner's scooter plunged down a flight of steps and crashed into a heap at the bottom. Skinner screamed in frustration.

He glanced up to see Remy looking down at him from the walkway, the documents still clutched in his mouth. Remy laughed with delight. Unfortunately, a gust from a passing bus swept the will away from Remy. The will floated high in the air, then fluttered over the river's edge. Skinner saw his chance. He climbed back aboard the moped and took off after the fluttering papers.

Remy chased the will from above, the letter still in his mouth. The will began to float down, heading right toward Skinner's grasping fingers. That was when Remy made two amazing, desperate leaps: one from the railing to a tree, the other from the tree to the floating will, which he plucked out of midair. Skinner watched in shock as Remy landed on the canvas roof of a passing riverboat.

Skinner leapt onto the deck of the riverboat. Remy, documents clenched carefully in his teeth, jumped to another passing boat. Skinner followed Remy, jumping from boat to boat until finally they were stuck on the same one. The next possible boat—a dining boat—was too far away for Remy to reach. Skinner laughed. The will was his! But Remy made the impossible leap anyway. The documents caught the wind, allowing Remy to land safely on the boat's deck. Skinner jumped after him, but he was not so lucky. He landed in the middle of the Seine!

An hour later, Skinner returned to his office. He was soaked and furious. He became even angrier when he discovered Linguini sitting at his desk. "You?" Skinner spluttered. "Get out of my office!"

"He's not in your office!" said Colette. "You are in his." She held up Gusteau's will.

Skinner gasped in disbelief. That *rodent*!

Linguini was the toast of the town. Journalists swarmed Gusteau's for a press conference. They all wanted a photo of the rising young chef and a quote or two for the next morning's edition.

"Chef Linguini," a reporter said, "your rise has been meteoric, yet you have no formal training. What is the secret to your genius?"

"Secret?" said Linguini. "You want the truth?"

Remy smiled and smoothed down his fur. He was finally ready for his big moment.

But Linguini didn't lift his hat and present Remy to the press. Instead, he said, "I . . . am . . . Gusteau's son. It's in my blood, I guess."

Remy was disappointed. And his frustration with Linguini only grew as Linguini fielded question after question from the reporters and never once mentioned Remy.

Linguini was cocky, sure of himself. He was no longer just the garbage boy.

Remy pulled angrily on Linguini's hair. Finally, Linguini took off his chef's hat with Remy inside and placed it on a nearby table. He didn't want Remy to distract him anymore.

Across the street from Gusteau's, a nervous, unshaven Skinner dressed in a tattered trench coat stepped into a phone booth. From the corner of his eye, he could see the line of customers that snaked around the block.

The phone rang in the drab and cluttered Ministry of Health office. "Health inspector," said

Nadar Lessard, turning from a pile of paperwork.

"I wish to report a rat infestation," Skinner said in a low voice. "He's taken over my rest—er, uh, Gusteau's restaurant."

"Gusteau's, eh?" said Lessard. "I can drop by." He opened his date book. "The first opening is in three months."

Skinner nearly dropped the receiver. "It must happen now! It's a gourmet restaurant!"

Lessard sighed. "Monsieur, I have the information. If someone cancels, I'll slot you in."

"But, but, the rat—you must—"

Lessard hung up. Skinner listened blankly to the dial tone.

Back in the kitchen of Gusteau's, the chefs were steaming—mad, that is. Horst looked at the clock, scowled, and turned to Colette. "It's past opening time," he said.

"He should have been finished an hour ago," Colette replied with an annoyed sigh.

Suddenly, the front door of the dining room swung open, revealing a tall, thin, forbidding man. It was Anton Ego. The press gasped.

"You are Monsieur Linguini?" asked Ego.

"Hello," said Linguini, terrified.

"Pardon me for interrupting your premature celebration," said Ego. "But I thought it only fair to give you a sporting chance, as you are new to this game."

"Game?" asked Linguini, puzzled.

"Yes," said Ego. "And you've been playing without an opponent, which is, as you may have guessed, against the rules."

The press furiously snapped and scribbled away.

"I will return tomorrow night with high expectations," Ego said solemnly. "Pray you don't disappoint me." And with that, he turned and walked out of the restaurant.

The press conference was over.

Before Linguini returned to the kitchen, he took Remy into his office. "You were distracting me in front of the press," he said, irritated. "How am I supposed to concentrate with you yanking on my hair all the time? And that's another thing. Your opinion isn't the only one that matters here. Colette knows how to cook, too, you know."

But Remy, who was sitting on Linguini's head, under his hat, was fed up. He grabbed Linguini's hair and pulled it as hard as he could.

*"Ow!"* Linguini cried. "All right, that's it!"

Linguini stormed outside. He got in Remy's face and said, "You take a break, Little Chef. You cool off and get your mind right. Ego is coming, and I need to focus."

Meanwhile, Skinner was on the roof of the restaurant, watching the whole scene. "The rat is the cook!" he said with a gasp.

As Linguini headed back inside, Skinner ducked down the fire escape.

Remy was furious at Linguini. He picked up a

bottle and was about to throw it against the wall when he came face to face with Emile and a group of other rats.

"I'm sorry, Remy," Emile said. "I know there are too many guys. I tried to limit—"

"You know what?" Remy interrupted. "It's okay. Dinner's on me. We'll go after closing time. Tell Dad to bring the whole clan."

That night, Linguini arrived at his fabulous new apartment, hoping to find Remy. Since Linguini was the new owner of Gusteau's, it was good-bye, hot plate; hello, Eiffel Tower view! "Little Chef?" he called. No answer. He went to Remy's bed, but it was empty. Linguini stared out the window sadly. Was his friend gone for good?

# Chapter 11

Gusteau's was closed for the night. In the dark kitchen, a loose outlet cover plate swung up, and Remy emerged from the wall. He looked around, then signaled behind him: the coast was clear. As Remy opened the door to the food safe, rats poured in through the hole. While the crack food-theft unit was raiding the safe, Linguini suddenly walked into the kitchen.

The rats froze in place. Yikes!

"Little Chef?" called Linguini. "Little Chef?"

Remy stepped out of the shadows.

"Hey, Little Chef," Linguini said with a sigh of relief. "I thought you went back to the apartment.

Then, when you weren't there . . . It didn't seem right to leave things the way that we did, so . . ."

Remy listened to Linguini distractedly, certain the rats would be discovered at any moment.

"Look," continued Linguini, "I don't want to fight. I've been under a lot of pressure. A lot has changed in not very much time, you know? I'm suddenly a Gusteau, and I gotta be a Gusteau or, you know, people will be disappointed."

Emile was hidden on a shelf high up in the food safe. He tried as hard as he could to stay still, but hunger won out. He just couldn't resist the juicy bunch of grapes hanging in front of him. Slowly, he leaned forward, put his lips around a grape, sucked it off the stem, and swallowed it whole. Yum! Then, he leaned forward for another.

Linguini continued his little speech. "You know, I've never disappointed anyone before, because nobody's ever expected anything of me. And the only reason anyone expects anything from me now is because of you."

Remy listened carefully to Linguini. He felt Linguini's pain; he really did.

"I haven't been fair to you. You've never failed me, and I should never forget that. You've been a good friend."

Straining to reach the last grape, Emile lost his balance and fell, then landed spread-eagle on the floor. "Oof," he groaned.

A small cheese wheel plummeted after him and landed right on his stomach. The grapes he had swallowed whole immediately began to fire from his mouth.

"The most honorable friend a guy could ever ask—" Linguini continued, until suddenly he was hit right in the face by the flying grapes.

"What is this? What's going on?" he yelled. He pulled the door to the food safe wide open and caught Emile and a few other rats red-handed.

His face a mask of shock and disappointment, Linguini turned to Remy as the rest of the rats made their escape.

"You're stealing from me?" Linguini said in disbelief. "How could you? I thought you were my friend. I spared your life! I trusted you!"

Gesturing, Remy tried to apologize and explain, but there was nothing he could do. Linguini grabbed a mop and jabbed it angrily at the small band of rats, backing them out the rear door and into the alley.

"Get out!" Linguini yelled. "You and all your rat buddies! And don't come back or I'll treat you the way restaurants are supposed to treat pests!" He slammed the door behind him.

Emile and Remy stared at each other. Emile broke the silence. "Wow. He didn't even try to kill us," he said admiringly. "You must be in solid with this guy!"

Django and the rest of the rat clan emerged from the shadows.

"You're right, Dad. Who am I kidding?" said Remy. "We are what we are. And we're rats." He looked at the kitchen. "Well, he'll leave soon."

Remy slowly turned away. Linguini's words had stung. He now knew where he stood with the person he had considered his best friend. "And now you know how to get in. Steal all you want."

"You're not coming?" asked Django.

"I've lost my appetite," Remy said sadly.

Regretfully, Django watched his son leave. Although things had ended exactly as he had predicted, he hated to see his son so disappointed.

The next morning, Linguini sat in his office, in the middle of a full-blown panic attack. Colette opened the door. "Today is a big day," she told him. "You should say something to them."

"Like what?" he asked.

"You are the boss," she reminded him. "Inspire them."

Moments later, Linguini began his pep talk to the kitchen staff. "Tonight is a big night," he said. "Appetite is coming, and he's going to have a big ego." Wait—that hadn't come out right. "I mean,

Ego. He's coming. The critic. And he's going to order. Something. Something from our menu."

The cooks exchanged confused glances. Colette covered her eyes. This was *not* the inspiration she had in mind.

Remy watched through the kitchen window. He sighed in frustration.

Linguini was starting to sweat. "And we'll have to cook it!" he explained. "Unless he orders something cold. Like a salad."

Remy sighed again. This was painful.

"Just can't leave it alone, can you?" a voice said behind him. Remy whirled around. It was Emile.

"You really shouldn't be here during restaurant hours," said Remy. "It's not safe."

"I'm hungry!" complained Emile. "And I don't need the inside food to be happy. The key, my friend, is not to be picky." He cleared his throat. "Observe." Emile lifted a tarp. Underneath was a large piece of cheese.

Instantly, Remy saw that the cheese was inside a trap. "No, wait!" he shouted. He ran to Emile and knocked him away. Unfortunately, Remy fell right into the trap and was caught.

"Oh, no!" moaned Emile. "Oh, no, no, no! What do we do? I'll go get Dad."

Suddenly, a shadow loomed over them. It was Skinner's. And Skinner was chuckling evilly.

Quick as a wink, Emile hid behind the garbage cans. Skinner picked up the trap, grinning from ear to ear. "You might be clever," he said. "But you're still only a rat."

In the kitchen, Linguini continued his pep talk gone awry. "Sure, he took away a star the last time he reviewed this place. Sure, it probably killed Gust—Dad. But I'll tell you one thing—"

Just then, Mustafa burst through the dining room door. "Ego is here," he announced.

Everyone froze. It was as if all the air had suddenly been sucked from the room.

Colette cleared her throat. "Anton Ego is just

another customer," she said. "Let's cook!"

It was just what everyone needed to hear. With a burst of energy, the chefs returned to work.

Back in the alley, Skinner placed the trap in the trunk of his car. He chuckled again. "So, I have in mind a simple arrangement. You will create for me a new line of Chef Skinner frozen foods. And I, in return, will not kill you."

Remy looked aghast. Skinner smiled and slammed the trunk shut. Remy grabbed the bars of his cage and shook them. He was trapped.

After perusing the menu, Ego snapped it shut and handed it to Mustafa. He spoke in a low voice. "Tell your chef Linguini that I want whatever he dares to serve me. Tell him to"—his voice became an evil hiss—"hit me with his best shot."

Mustafa scurried back into the kitchen.

Skinner, disguised in a trench coat and a beret, sat at a table just behind Ego. He snapped his fingers to summon a waiter, then jerked his head toward

Ego. “I will have whatever he is having,” he said, gleefully waiting for things to fall apart.

Inside Skinner’s trunk, Gusteau appeared. He studied Remy, taking in his dejected pose. “So . . . we have given up,” he said.

“Why do you say that?” asked Remy.

Gusteau looked around and shrugged. “We are in a cage. Inside a car trunk. Awaiting a future in frozen food products.”

“No,” Remy said, correcting Gusteau. “I’m the one in a cage. *I’ve* given up. You are free.”

“I am only as free as you imagine me to be,” said Gusteau. “As you are.”

Remy rolled his eyes. “Oh, please. I’m sick of pretending! I pretend to be a rat for my father. I pretend to be a human through Linguini. And I pretend you exist so I have someone to talk to! You only tell me stuff I already know! I know who I am! Why do I need you to tell me? Why do I need to pretend?”

Gusteau smiled. "Ah, but you don't, Remy." And then he faded away.

*Crash!* Something very large and heavy fell on the trunk of the car, creating a rat-sized hole.

"What the . . . ?" said Remy.

It was Emile! He, Django, and some of the stronger rats had toppled a stone gargoyle from a nearby building onto the car!

"Hey, little brother!" said Emile, climbing into the trunk.

Django was right behind him. Working together, the three rats managed to pop the latch holding the trap shut. Remy jumped out and gave his father and brother quick hugs. "I love you guys," he said. Then he jumped out of the car and ran down the alley.

"Where are you going?" Django called.

"Back to the restaurant!" Remy shouted over his shoulder.

"To save that kid?" Django asked.

"To save myself!" Remy yelled.

# Chapter 12

The kitchen was a madhouse. Orders were piling up. A platter of dishes crashed to the ground. A waiter slipped and fell. The kitchen was falling apart under Linguini's leadership.

Horst confronted Linguini. "It's your recipe!" he said, pointing to a pan filled with gray glop. "How can you not know your own recipe?"

"I didn't write it down," said Linguini. "It just . . . came to me!"

"Well, make it come to you again, ya?" said Horst. "Because we can't serve this!"

"We will make it," Colette said reassuringly. "Just tell me what you did!"

"I don't know what I did!" cried Linguini.

"We need to tell the customers something," said Horst.

The pressure was getting out of control. Linguini couldn't take another minute of it. "Then tell them . . . tell them . . . *agh!*"

Linguini ran into his office and slammed the door.

In the kitchen, Colette and Horst began arguing. Then Horst froze, his gaze fixed on the back door. There, standing in the middle of the doorway, as bold as bold could be, was Remy. He was ready to cook, and nobody was going to stop him.

*"Raaat!"* screamed Colette, Horst, and Lalo.

The chefs all seized various kitchen utensils and began to charge at Remy. But the little chef didn't move a whisker. Suddenly, a voice rang out.

"Don't touch him!" It was Linguini.

The chefs dropped their weapons and turned to stare at Linguini.

"I know this sounds insane," he said. "But—

well, the truth sounds insane sometimes, but that doesn't mean it's not the truth."

The cooks exchanged confused glances.

"And the truth is I have no talent at all. But this rat—he's the one behind these recipes. He's the cook. The real cook."

And right in front of the chefs' unbelieving eyes, Remy stood on his hind legs and walked over to Linguini, who lowered his palm so that Remy could hop onto it. Linguini lifted Remy to his head, then began picking up spices and holding them up to Remy's nose. The chefs murmured. So *that* was what he had been up to!

"He's been controlling my actions," Linguini explained to the mystified crowd. Remy then gave Linguini's hair a few tugs to demonstrate, and Linguini's limbs began to move.

"He's the reason I can cook the food that's exciting everyone, the reason Ego is outside that door. You've been giving me credit for his gift. I know it's a hard thing to believe, but hey, you believed I could cook, right?" Linguini let out a nervous laugh. "Look, this works. It's crazy, but it works. We can be the greatest restaurant in Paris. And this rat, this brilliant little chef can lead us there." He took a deep breath. "Whaddya say? You with me?"

For a moment, no one moved. Then Horst, tears welling up in his eyes, crossed over to Linguini. Linguini smiled at him gratefully—until Horst handed him his hat and his apron and left the kitchen, not uttering a word. Linguini watched, stunned, as one by one the rest of the staff resigned. Only Colette was left.

Colette was angry. She raised her hand as if to slap Linguini, but decided against it. Then she, too, walked out the door.

Linguini sighed deeply. His girlfriend had just abandoned him. He had no waiters, no chefs, and a roomful of hungry customers. And an important food critic to feed. It was all just too much for him. He looked at Remy, his eyes filled with tears, then turned and ducked into his office.

Remy stood in the empty kitchen, utterly alone. Just then Django stepped out of the dark shadows. He had witnessed the entire scene.

"Dad! Dad, I—I don't know what to say!" Remy cried.

"I was wrong about you," Django told his son. "About him."

"I don't want you to think I'm choosing this over family," Remy said. "I can't choose between two halves of myself."

"I'm not talking about cooking," Django explained. "I'm talking about guts. I couldn't do what you just did. I'm proud of you." He turned and let out a piercing whistle. The rest of the rat clan emerged from the shadows, quickly filling the kitchen.

"We're not cooks," said Django. "But you tell us what to do, and we'll get it done."

They heard a creak. And there at the back door was the health inspector. He stood frozen in shock, staring at the kitchen, which was crawling with rats. He slowly backed away and made a run for it.

"Stop that health inspector!" cried Remy. Django sent a squadron of his strongest rats to catch him. It was as good as done.

Remy got down to the next order of business: hygiene. By loading the rats into the dishwasher and choosing the light wash cycle, he got everyone clean and fluffy in no time.

Remy began shouting orders. "Team three will be handling fish; team four, roasted items; team five, grill; team six, sauces! Get to your stations! Let's go!"

When Linguini came out of his office, he was astonished. But he quickly joined the team. He strode up to Remy, suddenly filled with purpose. "We need someone to wait tables," he said.

Remy nodded.

Linguini grabbed his backpack and turned it upside down. A pair of roller skates fell out.

Moments later, clad in his blades and a waiter's outfit, Linguini burst into the dining room and began distributing menus to the diners with economical precision. "I'm sorry for any delay," he explained, "but we're a little short tonight."

Back in the kitchen, rats were sautéing, seasoning, and grilling up a storm. Remy raced around the room, overseeing everything. He tasted each and every dish before he deemed it perfect enough to leave the kitchen. Linguini glided back and forth between the kitchen and the dining room, delivering the meals.

Then the back door swung open. It was Colette. Her eyes nearly doubled in size as she surveyed the bizarre scene before her. Looking as if she might be ill, she turned to leave.

"Oh, Colette, you came back!" Linguini shouted. "Colette, I—"

She held up her finger to shush him. "Don't say a word," she said. "If I think about this, I might change my mind." She pulled on her apron and hat. "Just tell me what the rat wants to cook."

Remy flipped Gusteau's cookbook open and showed Colette the recipe he had chosen.

Suddenly, there was a loud screech of tires, followed by a crashing noise. A moment later, the back door swung open and the bound and gagged health inspector floated across the floor, supported by a bunch of rats. They quickly dumped him in the food safe. Colette barely even glanced up.

Just as she was about to put the very last ingredients into the ratatouille, she found her bowl blocked by a wooden spoon. Remy was holding it. He looked at Colette and made a face. With his spoon, he pointed to the ingredients he had collected himself.

Shaking her head in disbelief, Colette complied. Smiling, Remy finished the sauce and put the ratatouille on a plate. Linguini skated it into the dining room.

A hush fell over the room as the simple meal arrived at Ego's table. At the next table, Skinner received the same meal. "Ratatouille? They must be joking," he muttered. He glanced at Ego, who seemed equally unimpressed. As he watched Ego scribble a few notes in his pad, Skinner cackled to himself delightedly.

Linguini watched the critic, his eyes full of worry.

A bored look on his face, Ego poked his fork into the stew and brought it to his lips. But wait—what was this intoxicating aroma? As his mouth closed around the forkful of food, the sounds and sights of the restaurant faded away. The taste combinations were like a symphony. Memories began to swirl in his head. Suddenly, he was a little boy again and had just fallen off his bike. His mother took her sniffling son inside and gave him a plate of food to comfort him—a plate of ratatouille.

While Ego was lost in his reverie, his pen slipped from his hand. It clattered to the table, jolting him out of his memories. He blinked and looked down at the extraordinary stew. And for the first time in a very long while, Ego smiled. And then he helped himself to another mouthful.

Growing increasingly upset, Skinner watched the transformation on Ego's face. Then he himself took a forkful of the ratatouille. He loved the way it tasted; he hated it for being so delicious. "No . . . no, it can't be," he muttered.

Skinner burst into the kitchen, unable to take it anymore. "Who cooked the ratatouille?" he shouted. "I demand to know!"

The rats all stopped what they were doing and turned to look at him.

Skinner gasped. Moments later, he found himself being bound and gagged and placed into the food safe, right next to the health inspector.

In the dining room, Ego was nearly finished. He did what his mother had long ago told him never to do in public: he took one long, bony finger, dabbed the last smear of sauce from his plate, and brought it to his lips. Smiling broadly, Ego patted his lips with his napkin and turned to

Linguini. “I can’t remember the last time I asked a waiter to give my compliments to the chef,” he said. “And now I find myself in the extraordinary position of having my waiter *be* the chef.”

“Thanks,” Linguini replied. “But I’m just your waiter tonight.”

“Then who do I thank for the meal?” Ego asked, a bit confused.

Linguini stared at him for a moment, unsure of how to respond. He excused himself and returned with Colette.

Ego began to compliment Colette, but she stopped him. She was not the chef, either. Ego was now intrigued, and he demanded to meet the mystery chef.

After all the diners had left, Colette and Linguini brought out Remy, who looked slightly nervous. Ego laughed, thinking it was a joke. But Colette and Linguini assured him that it was not a joke at all. They told their story, Ego interrupting with occasional questions. And when the story was over, Ego stood, thanked them for the meal, and left without another word.

That night, no one—rat or human—could sleep as they anxiously awaited the next morning's review. Remy sat up all night long on Linguini's windowsill, staring at the Eiffel Tower.

The next day, the review appeared. Colette, Linguini, Remy, and the rat clan gathered in the kitchen to read it. And this is what it said:

> In many ways, the work of a critic is easy. We risk very little yet enjoy a position over those who offer up their work and their selves to our judgment. We thrive on negative criticism, which is fun to write and to read. But the bitter truth we critics must face is that, in the grand scheme of things, the average piece of junk is more meaningful than our criticism designating it so.
>
> But there are times when a critic truly risks something, and that is in the discovery and defense of the new. Last night, I experienced something new, an extraordinary meal from a singularly unexpected source. To say that both the meal and its maker have challenged my preconceptions is a gross understatement.

> They have rocked me to my core. In the past, I have made no secret of my disdain for Chef Gusteau's famous motto: Anyone can cook. But I realize that only now do I truly understand what he meant. Not everyone can become a great artist, but a great artist can come from anywhere. It is difficult to imagine more humble origins than those of the genius now cooking at Gusteau's, who is, in this critic's opinion, nothing less than the finest chef in France. I will be returning to Gusteau's soon, hungry for more.

Colette and Linguini embraced each other. Remy and the rat clan cheered.

The night before—running the kitchen, working with his family, taking one of Gusteau's recipes and making it his own, and pleasing the harshest food critic in France, if not in the world—had been a great night. It had been the happiest night of Remy's life, in fact.

The end? No way! Here's what happened next. They had to let Skinner and the health inspector loose and those two, well, ratted everyone out. The Ministry of Health closed down Gusteau's for good.

Remy, Linguini, and Colette were all unemployed. The rats no longer had a place to get quality food.

And Ego? Ego was fired. He'd never review another restaurant again.

The end? Guess again! Remy, Linguini, and Colette opened a bistro. Linguini served. Colette and Remy cooked. There was something for everyone: a small bistro in the back was for the rats, and a large one in the front was for the humans. The name? Le Ratatouille, of course! It became one of the most popular places in town.

And their most loyal customer? He was a tall, skinny former food critic turned small business investor with an intense love of ratatouille. It was in fact Anton Ego, and he came in for a bowl of ratatouille—sometimes two—every night. And soon, Anton Ego was skinny no longer!

Gusteau had been right. Anyone—regardless of upbringing, training, type of kitchen, or even species—could cook!

The end? You bet! Endings don't get much happier than this one!